The

Captives

By: Austin Swick

Text © 2014 by Austin Swick

Cover and interior design created by Austin Swick using
CreateSpace™

The Captives Publishing Rights © Austin Swick

All rights reserved. Published using CreateSpace™.

No part of this publication may be reproduced, stored in a
retrieval system, or transmitted in any form or by any means,
electronic, mechanical, photocopying, recording, or
otherwise, without written permission of the publisher.

ISBN-13: 978-1-494-96675-1

ISBN-10: 1-494-96675-1

Printed in the U.S.A.

4

This is a book…

Chapter 1

Fourteen years ago I, Curtis Lynch, was born into this world. Apparently, I was quite a large baby and had two monstrous eyes that were hazel-brown, just like my father's. My mother was almost the opposite of my father in appearance. My father was very tall and had darker features, such as stark black hair and, of course, hazel-brown eyes. My mother was quite short and had lighter features, including sky blue eyes and sunny blonde hair.

Ever since I was able to walk, I would go to play at St. Roy's Orphanage, an orphanage in my neighborhood, whenever both of my parents worked all day. The orphanage was like my second home. My parents could've put me in a daycare, but Emilia, the owner of the orphanage, and my parents were good friends.

I loved going to the orphanage. There were only about six children there at the time. My best friends there were Henry Young, Megan Blackwood, and Adam Brookson.

Henry was the youngest of us four, one year younger than Adam and I. He was somewhat Korean and had short hair that was as black as... black hair, for lack of a better simile. Henry always had his nose in a book, even as a child.

Megan on the other hand, was the eldest of us four, a little over a year older than Adam and I. She had flowing golden hair with blue eyes that continuously shined. She was also a very talented artist who could turn a blank paper into an intricate and flawless design.

Adam was a lively kid and was full of energy. He always wore the same necklace with a silver orb on the end of it, which matched his silvery-grey eyes. He constantly wondered how things worked and how they were made.

Emilia, the owner of the orphanage, was great with kids. She was good at entertaining, teaching, and pretty much whatever skills a person who worked with kids would need. She always held her orange hair in a bun, and many times she hung two golden hoops from her ears. She somewhat resembled Ms. Frizzle from the Magic School Bus.

I spent most of my time at the orphanage with Henry, Megan, and Adam even as I grew older. My mom said it wasn't really an orphanage, because Emilia had basically adopted kids that didn't have homes. Emilia had always wanted lots of children, so it worked out perfectly. None of the orphans really wanted to be adopted, because Emilia was so nice to them and they wanted to stay at the orphanage.

One of my favorite memories there was when Megan got glasses. We were all around the age of seven then, and we thought her pink glasses were super cool because when we put them on our vision became all messed up. Henry had this idea that we should all get them so that we'd look like spies on TV. Emilia said that we couldn't, but we could try making our own. The next day we made our own glasses out of cardboard (which Megan cut out for us because she was the only person that was good at art). We colored them with markers in our favorite colors and went on "spy missions" together. Adam owned his own spy kit and put it together all by himself, and Emilia couldn't even do that!

Probably my strangest memory was when I had just turned twelve. I remember it like it was about two years ago...

"Beep! Beep! Beep!" screeched my mom's alarm clock. I woke up and bolted over into my parents' room to turn off the alarm. My parents weren't in their room, so I figured they were already eating breakfast downstairs on the main floor. I hopped down the stairs two at a time and when I got downstairs, what I saw at the table was not my parents, it was a note:

Dear Curtis,

We will be staying somewhere else for a while. You will stay with Emilia at the orphanage until we get back.

Love,

Mom and Dad

The note looked like it had been written hurriedly. I was fine with it at the time, because it meant that I would get to see my friends every day. I was very confused as to why they never told me that they were leaving before hand, and they didn't state where they were going, or why they had to leave. Then I thought to myself it'll just be like a sleep over for a few days. I couldn't have been more wrong.

Chapter 2

(About 2 years later, present time)

"Happy birthday to you, happy birthday to you, happy birthday dear Curtis, happy birthday to yooouuuu!" I opened my eyes and saw Adam, Megan, Henry, Emilia, Lemmy, and the other three orphans standing around my bed. They were in my room in the orphanage. Morning sunlight flooded through the window and rested atop my bed sheets. Everything seemed to scream the word "peaceful".

Lemmy is an adorable eight year-old boy who has been living in the orphanage for about a year. He is quite small and has the funniest laugh you'll ever hear.

"There's the birthday boy!" Emilia squealed.

"I can't believe you are 14," Henry exclaimed. "You're a year older than you were 365 days ago!"

Later, I left my room and hopped down all three flights of stairs to get to the main floor where my breakfast awaited. On the main floor was the dining room, the living room and Emilia's room. Emilia's room was one of the coolest places you could be in the presence of. She specifically designed her enormous bed which stood about five feet above the ground. There was a majestic glass staircase that led up to her bed. It was like a room in the royal chambers of a king.

Emilia was amazing at design, because that was her job. She was the boss of her own home furniture design company called Hail's Furniture Design. (Hail is Emilia's last name.)

Emilia helped design all of our rooms. Henry's half of our room is based on books because

Henry loves to read. His writing desk is in the shape of a book and his file cabinet is an enormous book, each page being a different file holder. My side of the room is full of notebooks for me to write my stories in and has a small cubicle called "The Writing Room".

Megan's room, which is also on the third floor, is art designed which Megan actually helped Emilia construct. Adam's side of his room, which he shares with Lemmy on the second floor, is all mechanical and has a plethora of unnecessary, yet extremely cool, gadgets.

This might make Emilia sound rich, but she built all of it herself. The orphanage was an abandoned boarding home from a century, or so, ago. It was going to be torn down, but Emilia made it into the orphanage. That is why there are three floors and so many rooms. Every now and then we find a relic from the days when this place was

15

running as a boarding home such as a penny from 1902.

Our breakfast was turkey bacon and peanut butter waffles (my favorite breakfast), then we went sledding and had a snowball fight for a while outside. At one point we tied our sleds together with a rope and went down the steepest hill in our neighborhood. On our perilous sledding ride, our rope caught on a tree and snapped in half and we all went flying off our sleds down the hill. It was quite funny, and Emilia even got it on video.

After our rope snapped, we made snow forts as bases for our snowball fight. The teams were boys against girls, and last week the girls defeated us in the snowball war, which is not something that we are proud of. We were ready to get revenge. On the boys' team were Henry, Adam, Lemmy, Rick, Gabe, and I.

Rick is one of the orphans that is two years older than me and is like 6'5" or something. He doesn't talk all that much though, so there isn't much that we know about him.

Gabe is one of the workers at the West Shore Church, which neighbors the orphanage. He's the assistant Pastor, and the daycare worker. Gabe is really nice and funny and he always has a good joke to tell us. He visits the orphanage a lot, not so much for us, but for Emilia. Gabe and Emilia are engaged and are getting married soon in the church. I hope they get a giant cake!

On the other hand, the girls on the opposing team were Megan, Emilia, Katrina, and Marina. Katrina and Marina are twin sisters who are both nine years old. They are always following Megan around, and they adore her.

Okay, back to the story, we were getting prepared for the fight and we were almost done with our fort.

"Get the snowball launcher!" commanded Gabe to Henry and I.

"We gotcha," Henry replied. We scampered into the orphanage garage that smelled of fresh paint. We got the snowball launcher out of a cardboard box. The snowball launcher is basically just a little wooden catapult thingy that Henry, Megan, Adam, and I made many years ago. We lifted the strange catapult from the box and carried it out of the garage, just as Megan, Katrina, and Marina strutted in.

"Hey, you guys got the catapult last week," Megan said with her voice full of irritation.

"Yeah," Katrina and Marina said simultaneously.

"It's *my* birthday," I reasoned.

"Fine, take it," Megan said after a long pause. She walked out with Katrina and Marina following at her heels. She turned around and smirked as if she had just thought of something devious.

When we got back to the fort Adam, Lemmy, and Rick had already made a pile of snowballs. We helped make more snowballs with them for a while.

"We will win this war!" Gabe declared, which signaled the start of the war. It was chaos. The girls were chucking snowballs at us like there was no tomorrow. We were firing as fast as we could, but we were still losing. I had a plan, so I loaded the snowball launcher and was about to fire when I realized something. Where was Megan? Just then I felt a mountain of icy-cold snow being dumped on my head. I shrieked loudly and caught Henry's attention. He was sitting right next to me so he could hear me just fine, but everyone else was too far away and was focused on the commotion of the battle.

I turned around to see Megan backing away from me and moving towards Gabe holding a giant shovel. She refilled her shovel with snow and dumped it on Gabe's head. It was too late to warn him. He jerked violently and he turned around and started pelting Megan with snowballs. Eventually it got too cold for us to bear and we went inside to warm up and eat.

During dinner, Emilia brought in a chocolate covered cake with 14 candles and on it the words *Happy 14th B-day* scrawled across it and served us some hot chocolate with marshmallows. Adam loves chocolate, and Adam also loves cake. He was looking at the cake like a lion looks at it prey.

"Well, blow out the candles and make a wish!" said Megan.

I blew out the candles and wished that…

well; I'm not going to tell, because it's bad luck.

Everyone knows that. (It's pretty obvious what I

would wish for considering my circumstances.)

Henry and I were in our room, which we

shared, eating the cake and talking to each other.

"So," Henry questioned, "What did you wish

for?"

"Can't tell," I responded.

"Okay then, Curtis."

Adam and Megan came in and then the four

of us talked about random stuff while munching on

some delicious chocolate cake. Just then Adam

took one gulp of his steaming hot chocolate:

"HOT!! HOT!! HOT!! HOT!! HOT!!" he

sputtered.

"I'm guessing it's hot," Henry said. We all

died laughing. We decided to put our hot

chocolates out in the snow to cool them off, and Adam filled his mouth with snow.

"Ahhhhhh," Adam sighed in relief.

Later, I opened my presents. The first present I chose to open was from Emilia, it was 20 dollars. Emilia gives each of us 20 dollars every year for our birthday. Next, I got a bracelet with my name on it from Adam. After that I got a really big card from Megan that said "Happy B-day Curtis!" in 3D letters like those pop-up books and also had a cool drawing of Henry, Megan, Adam and I. Last, I got an emerald green notebook from Henry, because he knows that all of my other notebooks are full of all of my stories, and there is no room to write in any of them. I put all my presents in my bag and jumped into bed and drifted into a deep sleep.

Chapter 3

The next morning, I woke up to the sound of choirs of birds singing. It was a typical Sunday morning, I got dressed, ate, waited in the lobby for the other seven orphans and Emilia to wake up. At about 10:00, we strolled over to the West Shore Community Church.

Inside it is very lively and full of nice people. They have two large boxes of donuts every morning and Emilia has to tell Adam to only take one. Adam always picks the chocolate covered circular one with multi-colored sprinkles, but I like the glazed maple kind with chocolate drizzled on it. I'm sorry if I just made you extremely hungry. Today a man that I didn't recognize held out a box of donuts for us. There was just enough for us the seven orphans,

Emilia, and I. We all said thank you and headed towards the sanctuary.

"Do these donuts taste stale to you guys?" Megan asked.

"A little bit," Adam replied.

"What's a stale?" asked Lemmy.

"They're probably leftovers from last week," Henry said while Emilia explained what stale meant to Lemmy.

One of the people we always see there is Mrs. Adeline. She is a nice old woman who loves children and is always giving us candy and treats and such. Today she came up to us and she said she saw our rope snap in half when we were sledding and that she had an extra one that we could use. She pulled a slender rope out of her enormous violet purse.

"I have a feeling that you will need this," Mrs. Adeline said with a twinkle in her eye, almost as if she knew something that I didn't.

"Thanks a lot, Mrs. Adeline!" I exclaimed as she handed it over gently.

"Consider it a belated birthday present, Curtis" She replied with that same twinkle in her eye. I shoved it in my pack, which I take almost everywhere. Then we ran into Gabe.

"Hey kids!" Gabe exclaimed.

"Hey Gabey," Megan replied with a joking smile on her face, obviously thinking about the snowball fight.

"What a delight to see you." he mocked, and then laughed.

After church I strolled outside with Henry. The air was crisp and delicate snowflakes fell from the clouds.

"It feels like Christmas all over again," Henry said.

"Just nine more months to go," I replied. We were silent for a while as we walked down the empty street.

"Hey, I am really sorry about your house, Curtis," Henry said sympathetically after a long pause.

"Thanks," I said, "It's just that... It's just that I know that my parents will come back sometime." There was complete silence for a while. Henry looked as if he was pondering whether or not to say something.

"I never knew my parents. Well, I did but I don't remember them. They were murdered when I was only two," Henry said with sadness in his voice, "the murderer was never caught, and all that was ever found was a bronze locket with the word "nap" engraved on it. It just doesn't make sense, all of it."

This was all news to me. I had known Henry almost all my life, and I never heard this before. I knew that his parents were murdered, but I never heard any of the details. We reached my old house, which was about a block away from the orphanage. I stared at the red "For Sale" sign in the front yard.

"I can't believe that *my* house is going into foreclosure. How could they take this from me? Emilia told me that she begged the bank to keep the house just a little longer, but they said that that they were tired of waiting until my parents came back and that it was now going into foreclosure," I said, trying to hold in my frustration and sadness.

Just then I saw a slight movement out of the corner of my eye. I looked in that direction to see a man dressed in a strange black outfit looking through an Aniter (ANN-ih-terr) on a cliff about a half-mile away. An Aniter is a new form of technology that is basically a computer and a pair of binoculars combined, only better. It looks like a transparent blue mask that covers your eyes, and apparently they let you see for miles and miles, although I don't exactly know how the computer part works. My parents used to have two Aniters but I'm not sure how they could have afforded them because they cost about a fortune each. The strange man just stood there staring off in the distance, somewhere behind me. Then I realized something. He was staring at us.

Chapter 4

As soon as I blinked the man wearing the Aniter disappeared, as if he was never there in the first place. Was I going crazy?

"Hey Henry, did you see someone standing on that ledge over there?" I asked.

"No, why?"

"Never mind."

I must be going crazy I thought to myself. Seconds later, Adam walked up to us to join our conversation.

"Sorry to interrupt, but have you guys seen Megan anywhere?" Adam questioned.

"Nope. Did you already ask Katrina and Marina?" I replied.

"Yeah, but they hadn't seen her either."

"Maybe she already went back home." Henry suggested. He sounded kind of awkward when he called the orphanage "home".

Adam headed off towards the orphanage but we stayed at my house. Even though it technically wasn't my house anymore, we still ventured inside it. The only part I didn't like about coming back to my house, besides the memories of my parents, was that it felt empty. Too empty. What made my house look even more abandoned was the thin layer of dust that covered almost everything in my house.

"I haven't been in here in weeks," Henry said while wiping the dust off the wall.

"We'll this might be our last time," I said. Out of nowhere my head started hurting and I felt extremely light-headed.

"I think I'm going to pass out!" Henry said, grasping the wall.

"Me too," I exclaimed.

It suddenly became hard to breathe. My headache now felt like someone was trapped inside my head and was taking an enormous hammer and slamming it against my skull. I decided to get some water from the kitchen for us, because my dad always said that water helps headaches. It was extremely hard to walk. Everything seemed to be moving around me and my vision was blurred. When I came back into the family room, I thought that I saw Henry collapse onto the floor, but I couldn't be too sure if it was real or not. My headache pulsed at each heartbeat.

"Henry?" I called.

I tried to run over to him, but he was at the other side of the family room which seemed to stretch to about fifty feet away. The room started flooding with a strange looking orange water and it was pouring rain. I looked up to see how the rain was coming through roof of the house, but there was no roof. It had been torn completely off. The sky blazed the same shade of orange as the rain and the strange water that was flooding my house. Then Henry disappeared into the water.

"Henry, where are you? Henry!"

Suddenly, all the walls of my house were torn off by a huge tornado-like whirlwind of fire that now circled it. I could tell that something felt off about all of this, and that I was most likely hallucinating. The strange orange water was up to my waist. It was freezing cold. The house was floating up and up into the atmosphere. It was all happening so fast. Then my parents appeared.

"Just jump!" they said, "jump into the fire! Everything will be okay!" I jumped up as high as I could, but the water was sucking me in like a whirlpool. I could tell that my parents were not actually there because they looked almost like they were made of a clear blue mist. Almost like they were a projection.

"I can't do it!" I screamed, "I can't do it! Help me!"

My parents evaporated and so did my energy. I felt extremely sleepy. The world felt like it was spinning and shaking uncontrollably.

Then the water and fire formed a spherical ball around me and started spinning rapidly. I used all of my remaining energy to jump with all my might. I was successful this time. Oddly enough, everything froze in time.

Am I dying? Is this how it ends? The fire turned a shade of dark purple and disintegrated. The water turned into ice and then shattered into a million pieces and formed little snowflakes.

I must be hallucinating I thought to myself. Then all the snowflakes started to cover my shoes. Then my lower legs. Then my waist. I watched the snowflakes in horror, as I was unable to move. In a matter of seconds, the snowflakes had covered all of my body below my neck. They started to cover my mouth and I was too frightened and frozen in fear to scream. Next they covered my nose and it became even harder to breathe. After that, the snowflakes covered my eyes and the rest of my head and everything went black.

Chapter 5

When I woke up the last thing I could remember was that I was being engulfed by snowflakes. I sat up and looked for any sign of snowflakes covering me. I felt really shaky, like you do when you are really sick. There were none which made me feel a little relieved. It must have been a dream, right? Or maybe a hallucination. It's hard to remember some of it because when it happened I was half-awake and everything was all foggy.

My relief was gone when I came back to my senses and realized that I wasn't back in my house, or the orphanage. I surveyed and examined my current area. I was lying down on a comfy blue mattress that extended from the wall. I was in some sort of circular room. In the center of the room was a metallic slab that seemed like it was floating in midair; a table of sorts. Except it wasn't moving or shifting, it just floated motionless. On it was my bag, a tall cup of clear liquid, and two ripe apples. The clear liquid was most likely water, but I decided not to take the risk of drinking it. I did give in to eating one of the apples because I was starving. In less than a minute the apple core was all that was left. There was a glass window on one side of the room that was way too high to see through.

I wonder how long I have been unconscious for I thought to myself.

I walked over to a strange looking garbage can that seemed to be connected to the floor. An orange sign above it read *GARBAGE DISPOSAL*, as if it wasn't obvious enough. I pressed a button and the lid of it opened. I stared in awe at the endless pit before my eyes. Below where the bottom of the trash can would normally be was nothing; there was no bottom at all. I couldn't discern anything visible out of the blackness which made it very peculiar. I can see why they would have the sign there now, because it's hard to tell that the endless blackness is meant for garbage.

"Hello!" I yelled into it. My voiced echoed for a longer period of time than I have ever heard anything echo in my whole life. I dropped my apple core and waited for a plop or a splunk or something, but I didn't hear any noises.

I closed the lid of the strange can and looked around for any other interesting contraptions. Next to my bed was a similar button to the one on the garbage can. I pressed it which made the bed fold 90 degrees into the wall. I realized how silly I was being by admiring a trash can and looking around at the cool contraptions when I didn't even know where I was in the first place. I checked my bag, which rested on the floating table, and inside was my card from Megan, my journal from Henry, my $20 from Emilia, and my rope, which Mrs. Adeline gave me. I placed my bag beside my bed.

On the wall to the left was the word *IRIS* and a under it was a pink triangular button. I walked over to the wall and pushed the pink triangle. A large television screen popped out of a flap on the wall that was camouflaged to look like the rest of the wall. The screen blinked on and displayed a sky blue color. There were two animated eyes that blinked repeatedly before focusing on me. It looked as if hidden cameras hid behind those eyes. It also had an animated slit which I assumed was the mouth. It didn't have any other features though. No face, no nose, no ears. Just a pair of eyes focused on me and a mouth.

"Hello this is Iris speaking," it said in a female robot voice. The slit that I guessed was its mouth moved open and closed as it talked.

"Who are you?" I questioned.

"I am Iris the head of mechanical organisms of the Beneprobe Foundation."

"What's the Beneprobe Foundation?" I asked before she could continue. I was now sure now that it was a female.

"The Beneprobe Foundation is the head of the Advanced Technology Department in the CIA. Have you ever heard of an Aniter?"

"Yeah," I said, wondering how that question was relevant at the moment.

"I'm not surprised," she said, "They're all the rage these days. They were originally meant for CIA purposes only, but explorers and photographers seem to have a knack for these. Those aren't the only things made here. Some of the craziest inventions made here include thought pens, which write what you think, and negativitational rooms, which are rooms where everything is floating upside down and the gravity is opposite of normal." It made sense now why there is a floating table and an endless garbage disposal in my room. Iris continued, "Not to brag, but I am pretty revolutionary myself, I am the very first robot that makes its own decisions and can feel human emotions, except anger and hatred. I am one of a kind too," she said pompously. "They didn't show me to the public and didn't make any replicas, in case someone were to make a robot capable of harm and criminal activity."

"If the Beneprobe Foundation is part of the CIA, then why are you telling me all this? Isn't the CIA supposed to be all secretive?" I questioned.

"The fact is the Beneprobe Foundation really isn't what it used to be. I don't even think we should call it the Beneprobe Foundation anymore."

"Why?"

"Supposedly, a few years ago a large group of terrorists secretly joined the CIA somehow without anybody knowing. I think the part about them joining secretly is just a bunch of lies because it would be nearly impossible to pull that off with that large of a group. Well anyways, they convinced a lot of people to join them and they attempted to take over the Beneprobe Foundation by hacking. They were no match for us, but they had grown in numbers and had more people than us. They cut off our connection to the outside world and threatened to destroy everything, including our loved ones, unless we helped them. Not all helped, and most who didn't were killed. Now the Beneprobe foundation is taken over by terrorists. We have tried everything, but if anyone tells about these terrorists they will send all of our nuclear warfare bombs and weapons to countries across the globe. Who knows what will be left after that." She looked a little depressed when talking about it, if robots could be. To change the subject she said, "Enough about me, let's hear about you."

"I am Curtis, the human." I said

A small circular slot formed in the wall. Above it the words Place index finger in slot appeared. I put my finger in carefully, because who knows what could be in there. Then the words Registering fingerprint data... replaced the other words.

"I am registering you into my data files. You are Curtis Remy Lynch. Age: 14 years, 6 days, 10 hours, 12 minutes, and 32, no, 33 seconds old. Gender: Male. Parents: Alicia Rose Meyer Lynch, and Chuck Richard Lynch."

"So why am I here, and have I really been unconscious for four days?" She said that I was fourteen years and *six* days old. I remember blacking out the day after my birthday around noon. That's almost fourteen years and *two* days, not six.

"I don't know how long you have been unconscious. It is confusing to me as to why you are here also. I don't know why or how you got here either. I need to know what happened before you were unconscious." I told her about the hallucination that happened and the strange man with the Aniter.

"Someone is coming; don't tell them anything about me. No one that works here is trustworthy enough to know that I still run properly, and if anyone finds out they will shut me down for good, or worse." Iris said and retracted into the flap on the wall. The slot that was the fingerprint scanner disappeared. The pink triangle turned the same shade of white as the wall and retracted into it. The word *IRIS* disappeared as well. You could not tell that any of it had been there in the first place. It looked like a flat wall.

Suddenly, a tall girl with silver flowing hair appeared through a doorway that I thought before was just part of the wall.   I would've never guessed that it was a door. This made me wonder if there were more secret doors on any of the other walls.

"Hello my name is Nova," she said while avoiding looking at me, "When you are hungry, you can step into this elevator tube to go to the food area. Don't even try to escape because you are locked in from the outside." When she was done, she looked at me with an almost blank expression. I thought I saw sparkle of some sympathy in her eyes for a split second. Before I could ask a question, she walked out.

After a few seconds, the pink triangle appeared along with the word *IRIS.* I walked over to the button and pushed it, and sure enough Iris came out of the flap on the wall.

"Hello this is Iris speaking" She proclaimed. After she blinked a few times she focused on me. She looked like she knew what I was going to say, but I said it anyways.

"Iris... I am being held captive here."

Chapter 6

The words "held captive here" echoed in my head as I ate my dinner, which was soup, two days later. Nothing noteworthy happened on any of those two days, I spent most of the time sleeping, eating, talking with Iris, and looking into a garbage can. I was currently in the "food room", which was accessible by using the tube-like elevator in my room, which that Nova girl pointed out. The "food room" was puny in size, about half the size of my room/cell. All that was in it was a smaller circular floating table and a singular metal slab which also floated on air; which was supposed to be a chair. When I first sat down on it, I expected it to lurch down a bit under my weight, but it didn't even move a millimeter. I checked under it to see if there was a propeller lifting it, but there wasn't. I felt for invisible legs, but there weren't any of those either. Now, while eating my soup, I wondered how on earth this was possible, but I decided to drop the subject because there is probably some scientific explanation for it that I can't think of.

The only other objects of interest in the room where another endless garbage can and a machine that dispenses food. Before you get your hopes up, just know that the only food items you could get were a bowl of soup, an apple, and a bottle of water. The soup was basically a bowl of broth with some noodles floating at the top. I had already eaten my other apple earlier and drunk the clear liquid that turned out to just be water. A red sign on the wall read *Please place bottles and bowls in the garbage disposal*.

I realized how exhausted I felt and decided to go to bed. It was a long night. I tossed and turned, and even fell out of the bed once or twice. I didn't get to sleep for a very long time because I kept wondering why I would be held captive here in the first place. There were no clocks around, but it felt like I got about three hours of sleep at most.

When I woke up, I just laid there in my bed for a while trying to get back to sleep. About a half-hour later, I decided to give up on trying to get back to sleep because it was no use. My body wouldn't fall asleep.

After a while I became lonely so I got up talked to Iris.

"Hello this is Iris speaking," she said. She blinked a few times and then focused on me. "Curtis, one of my features is that I can monitor some of the hallway cameras in this building. I want you to see this footage I recorded of some of the terrorist people that work here."

A video popped up on to the screen, covering her face. It showed two people: the Nova girl and a man in a black suit. I thought that I had seen the black suit from somewhere before. They started to talk to each other.

"How many are awake?" the man said.

"Only one so far, sir. It's *him*," Nova said.

"Well… Did you interrogate him yet?"

"No sir, it's no use. Booker told me that the kid doesn't know a thing. His parents never told him."

"Then why is he here!" the man exclaimed.

"By the time I had realized that he knew nothing, it was too late." A deep ominous voice said. A person in the same black suit walked out of the shadows and into the light. Now he was visible. He had a long pointed nose and eyes of a bloodthirsty snake that sent chills through my body. I thought that I recognized this guy from somewhere. But where? That question was nagging at the far end of my brain, as if looking for the answer in a game of hide and seek. How did I know this guy? I definitely didn't personally know him or his name for that matter. Had I seen him somewhere? Yes, I think so. But where? I stared at the guy intensely, as if that would tell me the answer. Then it hit me. The question in the back of my brain found the answer it was seeking.

It was the guy that was staring at me and Henry with the Aniter after church. The one I thought I saw disappear. Maybe I wasn't crazy and he actually disappeared. A second wave of chills ran up my back and made me shudder. The recorded footage ended and I was still standing there shocked. Then Iris said something much, much scarier than that man in black.

"Curtis, I think they are talking about you."

Chapter 7

It felt like my head was spinning at an uncharted speed. If those people were really talking about me, were they really talking about my parents? They've been missing for two years! For all we know, they could be... you know. And what was it that my parents never told me? What were they going to interrogate me about, before they realized that my parents never told me it? These questions were hurting my head and I tried not to think about my parents or any part of this conversation, but my brain wouldn't let me. I told Iris about the man that I saw wearing the Aniter.

About three minutes passed and I stood there motionless trying to comprehend what just happened in the footage that Iris showed me.

"Curtis, I must leave you, but I will be back in approximately… actually, I don't know how long I'll be gone." Iris said and then retracted into the wall along with the pink triangle. Her name under it disappeared too. It now looked like a normal wall once again.

I lied down on my bed and thought. I just lied there thinking for who knows how long. I closed my eyes and fell asleep. For about three hours I slept, and dreamt.

When I woke up, I was starving so I used the tubular elevator to go up to the food room. I pressed the *Soup* button and then the *Water* button. I chugged all of the water in the bottle at a record time of less than five seconds. I ate the warm soup slowly, savoring each gulp. I remembered how Emilia would make warm soup for us on cold winter days. Speaking of Emilia, where was she? And where were Henry, Megan, and Adam? What about the other orphans and Gabe? Surely they weren't here, right?

I took my bowl and went down through the elevator back to my room. Iris still wasn't back yet. What on earth could be taking her so long? There was one floating slab of a chair that I sat on as I finished my soup at the table in the center of the room. When my bowl was empty I moved my hand up to wipe my mouth, but as I did this, I accidentally hit the metallic soup bowl off the table. A split second later, I heard a loud *CLANG!* The bowl clearly hadn't broken if it made that kind of noise. That was the sound of a metal object hitting a metal floor. I looked over and saw a huge dent on the side of it. It was rolling on its side in a circular motion. It rolled under the table and fell on its bottom, facing upright, as if someone had put it there on display.

I was about to grab the bowl and throw it away when the table started to wobble. It would jerk up about two inches and then move back down to its original height. It moved in this pattern over and over again. I grabbed the bowl and pulled it out from under the table. The jerking stopped. The table was motionless now at its original height.

"That's odd." I said to no one in particular.

I placed the bowl back under the table, and sure enough it started to move up and down again. I took the bowl out from under the table and it stopped moving. I climbed onto the table and stood on it. It didn't budge a single millimeter. I jumped as hard as I could and landed with full force on the table. It didn't move at all.

How is this possible? I thought to myself.

I jumped off the table. Iris still wasn't back yet.

For the next eight hours, I did a lot of sitting around doing nothing. Some of the other things I did were eating lunch and dinner and making four tick-marks on the wall to count how many days that I have been here. Best of all, I put three bowls under the table and jumped up onto it and imagined that I was surfing on the ocean. Every time the table moved up, I was going over a wave. Because there were three bowls, the table was more wobbly and it moved higher up at a faster speed. I fell off it a few times, but I never got hurt. After the eight hours, I felt really tired and decided to call it a day. Just when I was about to jump into bed, the pink triangle appeared and then everything else followed. I ran over to the wall and pushed the triangle and surely, Iris pooped out.

Iris emerged from the flap in the wall. Blinked a few times and looked at me.

"Hello, this is Iris speaking," she proclaimed.

"Why were you gone so long?" I questioned.

"Curtis, I found another humanoid being who is being held captive here too. He is in the room right next to yours."

"What's his name?" I asked. Images of Henry collapsing onto the floor of my house during my hallucination popped into my mind. Maybe he had been taken here too. Maybe he was in the room right next to mine! But Iris said a different name than the one that I was thinking of.

"His name is Lemmy," she said.

Chapter 8

Lemmy! How in the world did little Lemmy get here? Maybe it was a different Lemmy. To make sure it was the Lemmy that I knew I asked Iris.

"Hey Iris, is his name Lemmy Cartinger?"

"How do you know his last name? I haven't even told you it yet! Using my superior logical ability to comprehend certain situations, I am inferring that you know Lemmy Cartinger personally. Am I correct?" she asked.

"Yes."

"Obviously my sublime use of intellect is unmatched." Iris said pompously. Instead of trying to figure out what she was even saying, I changed the subject.

"How did you find out that he is here?" I questioned.

"Well, I can see all of the footage through all of the cameras around this building. At first, I thought that the room next to you was empty, but Lemmy was there the whole time! I just didn't know it because he has been unconscious all this time and was covered up by his bed sheets. You were covered by yours too, except, I knew you were there the whole time because you kept jerking around as if you were trying to escape your endless sleep. Well, when Lemmy finally awoke today, I saw him and moved myself, my pink triangle button, and all of my other apparatuses from your room to his room. That's why I was gone for so long. I talked to him for quite a while. He asked a lot of the same questions that you did," she said.

"Well, I think that it would be best if I got some sleep," I said.

"Right, sleep. Sleeping always sounded boring to me. It sounds like a long time where you're powered off, except you are subconsciously dreaming. I don't understand why humans dream if you only remember your dreams about 22.3 percent of the time," she exclaimed. I think she rambled more about this for a while, but I was already asleep. I fell asleep almost the instant that my head hit the pillow.

I dreamed a very strange dream. I was running as fast as I could through a very large deserted room. Iris's voice spoke to me. I couldn't hear what she was saying because it sounded all muffled and distant. Iris didn't appear to be anywhere in particular either. I exploded through a set of glass doors out into the sky. I kept running. Nothing could stop me; I was like a meteorite soaring through the atmosphere. A pathway formed out of clouds. It became clear what I was running from. A vicious pack of bloodthirsty snowflakes. I continued sprinting. When I got to the edge of the path of clouds I jumped.

Chapter 9

Have you ever felt like you were falling down an endless pit of darkness? Knowing that you will never stop falling? Then there's the feeling of being encased by an endless blackness. It never stops. But then out of nowhere, you see the ground about 100 feet away. It grows ever closer. You are plummeting towards the ground, no way to stop. Now it's 50 feet away. Now it's 40. 30. 20. 10. You close your eyes right before you hit the ground and BAM! You wake up.

That's how I felt. I woke up frightened and sweaty, not a good combination. I guessed that Iris was gone again, by the normal-looking wall where she had resided earlier.

When Iris came back, I decided to show her the crazy bowl-and-table thing. I placed one bowl under the table and the table started to wobble and move up and down. I placed the next two under it and it started to move up to a higher height than it did with only one bowl.

"How did I not guess this earlier?" Iris said to herself.

"What?" I asked.

"I just figured out how the table floats in midair! It's a magnet!" she said, "There must be magnets in the floor that are repelling it so that it stays at the same height!"

"Iris, you're a genius!" I exclaimed.

"Thanks for the clarification of the obvious," Iris said jokingly.

"I wonder how high it could go." I said.

"Curtis, I am currently recording footage right now of the man you told me that you saw wearing the Aniter," she said. I walked over to her and the live footage now displayed on her screen/face. This time there were four men in black suits and the guy that I saw wearing the Aniter was there too.

"I need to tell you four a secret that you must not tell anybody else," the Aniter man said to the four men, "We have found Verena."

"Who?" One of the four men asked.

"Verena Blackwood. The leader of the Advanced Technology Department of the CIA. The leader of the Beneprobe Foundation." The Aniter man said. I heard Iris gasp.

"Blackwood is Megan's last name!" I thought to myself. Could they be related? Is that Verena person her mother? I focused back on the footage.

"We used the Truth Harness on her to get all the information about where the rest of the original CIA workers of the Beneprobe Foundation were now. Talk about giving her a taste of her own medicine, since she was the lead inventor of the

Truth Harness. Pike, Maxfield, and Ambrosia were sent to go retrieve all of the former Beneprobe workers from their little hideout. They should be coming back soon with all of them. Then we are going to transport all of the former workers to Sector 1 along with the kids."

"What about Chuck and Alicia's boy?" one of the men asked. This was the man that was talking to Nova and the Aniter guy in the other footage Iris showed me a while ago. He was talking about me!

"My parents were named Chuck and Alicia!" I yelled at Iris.

"He will stay here along with Young's kid," the Aniter man said. Young was Henry's last name! First Megan, then me, and now Henry! This was starting to scare me.

"Sir, Pike has landed and Ambrosia and Maxfield are on their way," one of the men in black said while getting off his phone.

"Perfect, we have the kids ready to be transported," the Aniter man said. The footage closed and now the screen displayed the usual, Iris's animated eyes and mouth. Before I could speak, Iris spoke.

"This is bad. Not bad, terribly bad! Be right back." Iris said. She contracted into the wall and her name and pink triangle disappeared. About ten seconds later she appeared again.

"Lemmy is gone!" she said. She must have seen how confused I looked by all of this so she tried to explain it.

"Curtis, the terrorists that have taken over this place have found the safe-haven where all of the former Beneprobe workers have hidden. They are taking them to another place called "Sector 1."

"Iris, they said something about a person named Verena Blackwood. One of my best friends was named Megan Blackwood, and her mom was killed in a car accident. I wonder if that was a lie, and that Megan's mom was Verena Blackwood, and if she went into hiding with the rest of the former Beneprobe workers," I said, " I also know who they were talking about when they said 'Young's kid'. They meant my friend Henry, he must be here also."

"Curtis, we don't have much time. You have to get onto one of the transporters and escape!"

"Why?" I inquired.

"Because they will kill you and your friend Henry if you stay here. They don't need you. Don't you see! Earlier they were talking about how they couldn't interrogate you because you didn't know anything that could help them! They are going to kill you, Curtis!" She yelled.

"How do you expect me to sneak onto one of those transporters unseen? How am I even supposed to get out of this room!" I questioned.

"Magnetics," she said.

Chapter 10

"Curtis, go get approximately four more soup bowls," Iris commandeered. I went up to the food room and ordered four more bowls. I dumped out the soup into the endless garbage can and went back down into my room. I put the bowls under my table. The table moved up all the way to the height of the window. I now saw how Iris wanted me to get out. I had to go through the window.

"Bye, Iris," I said.

"Are you kidding me? I would never let you go without me!" Iris said. She contracted into the flap on the wall. A few seconds later a small hole formed in the wall. Out came a square like device, about the size of a cell phone. The screen was sky blue and had two animated eyes and an animated mouth.

"How do you like my new form," she said, "I call it the Iris Mini."

"It's great," I said. I put her in my pocket.

I grabbed my pack off of my bed and jumped onto the table. It wobbled and jerked rapidly, so it was hard to get a good grip with my feet. I lost my balance and fell off it onto my back. The wind was knocked out of me, so it took a while for me to catch my breath. Once I did, I hopped back onto the table for a second attempt. No luck. I was thrown off it once more. This table felt like one of those machine bulls at the circus that Henry and I went to last year. Henry! He was here right? The people in the black suits said 'Young's kid'. Young is Henry's last name.

"We don't have much time!" Iris yelled. I jumped onto the table and steadied myself long enough to rise to the maximum height that the table floated. I needed something to attach onto the knob on the window and pry it open. It was unreachable no matter how high I jumped. The window was gargantuan; about six feet tall and ten feet wide. The bottom of it was a jump away from me, but I doubt that I could break through it. I needed something long, like a rope. A rope! I dug through my pack and grabbed the old rope that Mrs. Adeline had given me. I immediately tossed my rope towards the knob at the top of the window. The rope hit it like a whip, and I saw the knob move to the left a little. I whipped it again and it moved a little more. This time I heard a barely audible clicking noise that sounded like something being unlocked. The table was moving downwards, slowly this time. I had to time my jump just right.

"Jump!" Iris yelled. I did. I jumped. I slammed into the window, now unlocked, which opened outwards sending me falling about ten feet to the ground. Luckily, I landed on my feet.

Unluckily, it felt as if I had twisted my ankle, which most likely happened.

"Your friend should be in one of these rooms," she said. From the outside, I could see a black door on the front of my room, but on the inside of my room, it looked like a part of the wall. Next to the door was a name. CURTIS R. LYNCH. On the door seven feet to the right of mine read VACANT. This was Lemmy's room; I know this because there were no doors to the left of mine. I didn't have time to check inside Lemmy's room to see if it was identical to mine. I ran past six more vacant rooms until I got to a door with a name on it; HENRY J. YOUNG. I walked up to the door. There was no doorknob present so I assumed that it was a push door. I reached out my hand to touch it.

"Unknown fingerprint," a startling computerized voice said. I tried again. "Unknown fingerprint," it said once again.

"It's no use," Iris said. Out of nowhere Nova walked around the corner. I froze in fear. She kept walking as if she didn't even see me. She walked up to the door and placed her finger onto the door.

"Finger print data recognized," the monotonic robot voice said. Nova walked away from the door and turned to go around the corner. Before she moved completely out of my sight she looked straight at me.

"Save your friend," she said. She walked away. Just like that she was gone.

Chapter 11

I ran into the room, expecting to see Henry, but he wasn't even there! From two years of experience of sharing a room with him, I knew that he was exceedingly messy. His room was identical to mine. It couldn't have looked more different due to how messy and unorganized everything appeared. This room had to be his because it looked like a tornado had just come through and made a mess of things. Why wasn't he here? Where could he be!

"Henry!" I yelled, "Henry, where are you?"

"Shhh! We have to be quiet," Iris whispered. He had to be here! Those men in the black suits specifically said he was staying here. I analyzed the area. Could he have jumped into the garbage disposal? I doubt it because he wouldn't have fit through the opening. Where else could he have gone? Did he escape on his own? I looked around for clues of his location. Something shiny caught my eye. The tubular elevator! I sprinted into it and rode it up to the food room and jumped out when it reached the top. I heard someone fall over. I looked up to see a boy with black hair pointing a water bottle at me as if it were a sword.

"Henry, it's me, Curtis!" I half said and half yelled in fear of getting whacked in the face with a water bottle.

"Curtis?" he asked looking relieved. He lowered his water bottle. "You scared me half to death!"

"I'm sorry about that, but we have to leave now," I said.

"Why?" Henry questioned. Iris explained everything. At first he was a little concerned that a computer could have a conversation with us, but he got used to it.

After she explained the current situation Henry looked quite shocked.

"Hmph," he grunted in agreement.

"Our time is running out, we have to go now if we want to live!" I exclaimed. We rode the elevator down to his room and exited through the door which was still open.

"I never would've known there was a door there!" Henry said aloud.

"Shhh!" Iris whispered "We have to be quiet or else we might be caught."

We left his room and passed probably twenty more vacant rooms when we arrived at a breathtakingly (quite literally, if you climbed all the way up it) massive staircase that seemed to stretch on forever and ever. I was definitely not in any shape to use stairs considering my injured ankle.

Instead, we took the elevator which was conveniently placed right next to the staircase. We didn't even press a button, it just started moving up. Iris said it only had one destination, so there was no need for a button. It was probably the longest elevator ride that I ever had. I could tell it was moving exceedingly fast because my stomach dropped as if I was on a rollercoaster. We must have traveled at least four hundred feet upwards.

When we finally arrived at our destination a robotic voice spoke.

"Ground level," it said. *If this was ground level, my room must have been four hundred feet, or more, underground* I thought confusedly. It didn't feel like I was that far underground, but I guess there's no way to tell.

"That elevator over in the top right corner of this floor will take us to the Skytip." Iris explained, "The Skytip is the 29th floor of this building. The transporters' landing zones are on the outer balcony of the Skytip. That's where we need to sneak on board." I now acknowledged the tremendous size of the floor that I was on. It was almost like the size of a floor at a mall. There were four escalators, two going up onto the upper part and two that were going down from the upper part to the lower section that we were on. We dashed across the floor and hopped onto one of them which took us to the upper level. Next we sprinted to the right corner of the upper level, towards the elevator. I was having a hard time running because of the pain coming from my ankle, so I half-hobbled and half-ran. When we reached the elevator Henry and I leapt into it. This time, there were actual buttons so I pressed the button that had the number 29 on it. The elevator ride paled in comparison to the one we had recently experienced, only minutes ago.

We arrived at the Skytip in no time at all. It was an even bigger floor than the ground floor. The size of it was almost overwhelming to look at. It had a huge dome-shaped ceiling that seemed to be made of pure glass, except every once in a while I thought that I saw a flicker of a strange blue electric current running through it. I had to focus on running as fast as I could, which was excruciatingly painful because of my twisted ankle. I tried to ignore it as best I could. Every time that I stopped running it throbbed, sending pain shooting up my leg, which motivated me to keep running. I was breathing heavily and what made it worse was that I hadn't drunk any water since the night before, and I could feel my dehydration. My throat was dry. My foot hurt every single time that it touched the ground.

I could see the glass doors that opened out to the balcony that Iris talked about. We reached the doors and ran through them. The balcony was magnificently beautiful. It seemed to be entirely composed of pure gold. It was so shiny that I could see our reflection through it as we ran along it. Then I saw it. A large white hovercraft that resembled an oversized helicopter. There was a circular landing zone that branched off from the balcony. That's where it was parked.

"Hurry and get on that hovercraft! It's about to depart!" Iris screamed. Henry and I ran along the path from the balcony to this landing zone. The balcony was about 150 to 200 feet in the air, and it made me nauseous to think about. I tried not to look down over the golden banister that protected me from falling to my death. Henry and I were now thirty feet from the hover craft. I could see lots of people in it, but I couldn't make out any of their faces. There was an opening on the side of the hovercraft, so we would have to get on through there. What if they saw us? What if one of the terrorist shut the doors of the opening before we could get onboard?

I was worrying about all the things that could go wrong, and I wasn't paying any attention to where I was going. My bad foot slammed into the side of balcony and I fell onto my stomach onto the banister. I was about six inches from falling to my death.

"Curtis! Get up! We don't have much time!" Henry screamed over the noise of the hovercraft's engine starting. If the engine was starting that means they were seconds from departure. Henry and I sprinted as fast as we could. Iris was yelling something, but neither of us could hear it over the engine noise. We were fifteen feet away.

I saw the pilot in the cockpit. He was a tall man that had a huge scar running down the right side of his face. I could tell that he saw us coming he started the odd looking propellers on both sides of the vehicle. I knew that scar from somewhere. But where? The man that held out the box of donuts for us in the church! The guy who gave us the stale donuts!

All of these facts about the man with the scar started swirling in my head and connecting to each other like the pieces of a puzzle being solved.

There were exactly enough donuts for all of us orphans Emilia in that box. Normally we just grabbed a donut from the boxes on the counter, but this time the scar-guy specifically held out a box for us. Why? He wanted us to eat those specific donuts. Those donuts must have been drugged so that we would pass out and he could take all of us here. Wait a second; if he gave donuts to all of us then did he take us all here? The only other person that I knew of that was taken here was Henry. What about Lemmy? Did he black out too? I remember

Adam said he was looking for Megan that day; had she already been taken?

We were about five feet away when the vehicle lifted off the ground. We were almost directly under it now. It started to move away from us and was slowly flying over the edge of the balcony. This was our only chance. It was now or never. We had almost reached the edge of the balcony. There was no banister holding us back from falling 200 feet to our death this time. The vehicle's door was beginning to close.

That's when I saw them. Two people I knew very well. The man was rather tall and had stark black hair and hazel-brown eyes, like mine. The woman was much shorter and had light blue eyes and curly blonde hair. They had duct tape over their mouths and had some sort of green mechanical bindings on their arms and legs. The woman looked at me wide eyed and I saw a tear roll down her cheek. How I could not recognize them, I had thought about them every single night since they left two years ago.

The hovercraft door was only about four feet in front of our faces. After seeing them, it made me run even faster, forgetting the constant pain in my foot. I could tell that Henry recognized them too.

We didn't stop running. We got to the very edge of the balcony and did the unthinkable without any hesitation.

We jumped.

About the author

Hello readers, my name is Austin Swick. I am a twelve year-old boy who lives in the freezing cold land of Minnesota. I have loved to write stories since I was three. I have always wanted to be an author, and now for the first time in my life I can finally say that I actually am an official author. My favorite authors are Suzanne Collins, the author of "The Hunger Games" series and more, and J. K. Rowling, the author of "Harry Potter" series and more. Thanks for reading!

Keep an eye out for my upcoming sequel!

86

Made in the USA
San Bernardino, CA
21 March 2015